I'm Always Loving You

Kathy Wolff

illustrated by **Acamy Schleikorn**

BLOOMSBURY
CHILDREN'S BOOKS
NEW YORK   LONDON   OXFORD   NEW DELHI   SYDNEY

BLOOMSBURY CHILDREN'S BOOKS
Bloomsbury Publishing Inc., part of Bloomsbury Publishing Plc
1385 Broadway, New York, NY 10018

BLOOMSBURY, BLOOMSBURY CHILDREN'S BOOKS, and the Diana logo are trademarks of Bloomsbury Publishing Plc

First published in the United States of America in December 2024
by Bloomsbury Children's Books

Text copyright © 2024 by Kathy Wolff
Illustrations copyright © 2024 by Acamy Schleikorn

All rights reserved. No part of this publication may be reproduced or transmitted in any form
or by any means, electronic or mechanical, including photocopying, recording, or any
information storage or retrieval system, without prior permission in writing from the publisher.

Bloomsbury books may be purchased for business or promotional use. For information on bulk
purchases please contact Macmillan Corporate and Premium Sales Department at
specialmarkets@macmillan.com

Library of Congress Cataloging-in-Publication Data
available upon request
ISBN 978-1-5476-1420-2 (hardcover) • ISBN 978-1-5476-1421-9 (e-book) • ISBN 978-1-5476-1422-6 (e-PDF)

Art created digitally with Procreate on an iPad
Typeset in Humana Sans ITC Std
Book design by Yelena Safronova
Printed in China by Leo Paper Products, Heshan, Guangdong
2 4 6 8 10 9 7 5 3 1

To find out more about our authors and books visit www.bloomsbury.com and sign up for our newsletters.

To Mom and Dad, who are
always loving me.
—K. W.

To my son and daughter—
I'll always love you!
—A. S.

I love you when you rise and shine—
awake as you can get!

I love you when I haven't even had my coffee yet!

I love you when you brush your hair and try out something new,

when you've got a case of sillies,
and I catch those sillies, too!

I love you when the answer's yes,

and also when it's *no* . . .

. . . when we're sitting sorta quiet
or we need to go-go-go!

I love you at a traffic light,

I love you at the store.

I love you in the longest line we've ever seen before!

. . . when things are super *extra* great . . .

or go a little wrong.

I love you when you're close to me, and also when you're not,

and no matter what I'm doing,
I sure think of you *a lot!*

I love you on a twisty slide!
I love you on a swing!

I love you when you're off exploring every little thing!

I love you when you're helping out with dinner or with chores.

I love you eating tuna fish
(or better yet—*s'mores!*).

I love you when we're snuggled up
all cozy with a book,

when you're feeling kinda yawn-y
and you've got that droopy look.

I love you when you're jammied up,
all set to get in bed.

I love you when we hug
and when I kiss your sleepy head.

I love you when I say, "good night," and turn the light out, too.

And then, when you are sound asleep . . .

. . . I'll *still* be loving you!